for Mum

First edition published by Book Island August 2019
Second edition published November 2019
Third edition published January 2020
This paperback edition published 2021

Text and illustrations © Jayde Perkin 2019

Edited by Victoria Millar
Design by David Rose
Printed in Latvia

British Library Cataloguing-in-Publication Data
A CIP record for this title is available from the British Library.

Paperback edition ISBN: 978-1-911496-19-9
Hardback edition ISBN: 978-1-911496-13-7

Book Island would like to acknowledge the support of bereavement charities **Cruse Bereavement Care Bristol** and **Let's Talk About Loss** towards the production of this book. Visit **crusebristol.org.uk** and **letstalkaboutloss.org** to read more about the wonderful work they do with people who've lost a beloved one.

Book Island is a small, independent publishing house, based in Bristol. Visit **bookisland.co.uk** for more information about our picture books.

Mum's Jumper

Jayde Perkin

BOOK ISLAND

"Visiting hours are over," said the nurse.

"We love you,"
we told Mum.

We left the hospital and I wished
that Mum could join us.

Her favourite flowers lined the streets.

The next morning,
the phone rang.

It was the
hospital.

"She's gone,"
they said.

"Gone where?"
I asked.

It didn't feel real.
Nobody pinched me.
But if they did,
I'm sure I wouldn't
have felt it.

It was cold. I felt tired.

But I couldn't sleep.

The next few weeks were blurry.
Many people brought us cards and flowers.

Everyone would say, "I'm so sorry."
But it wasn't their fault.

There was a funeral.
There were more flowers.
There were more "I'm sorry"s.

There were also sandwiches,
but nobody wanted to eat them.

A dark space began to
follow me around.

I found it hard to
concentrate at school.

The sounds and voices around me
were distant and floaty.

My body ached, like I'd been swimming for days; how could I get to the shore?

Dad told me this feeling is normal.

It's called grief. He was swimming too. We were grieving together.

The teachers and my friends at school
were all really kind...

...so I couldn't understand
why I still felt so alone.

Sometimes I even felt angry that my friends
had mums who picked them up from school.

Dad and I slowly began to sort through Mum's things. Why would she leave them all behind?

She loved this jumper.

I love it too.

It smells like her.

Over time
it began to smell
like me instead.

And later Dad put
it in the wash.

Some people say that grief gets smaller over time.

But Dad says it's a little more complicated than that.

Dad says the grief is like Mum's jumper.

The jumper stays the same size,
but I will eventually grow into it.

The grief may stay
the same size.

But my world will grow
bigger around it.

I, too,
will grow.

I put the jumper in a drawer.
I don't need to wear it every day.

But I like to know it's there.

I feel Mum everywhere.
She's in the air, and in the sea,
she's in the flowers, and in me.